D1095285

Redworld is published by
Stone Arch Books, A Capstone Imprint
1710 Roe Crest Drive
North Mankato, Minnesota 56003
www.mycapstone.com

Library of Congress Cataloging-in-Publication Data
Names: Collins, A. L. (Ai Lynn), 1964- author. | Tikulin, Tomislav, illustrator.
Title: Raiders : water thieves of Mars / by A.L. Collins ; illustrated by Tomislav Tikulin.
Description: North Mankato, Minnesota : Stone Arch Books, a Capstone imprint, [2018] |
Series: Sci-finity. Redworld ; [2]
Summary: In 2335 the most precious resource on Mars is water, and Water Raiders are
    attacking farm communities and stealing the water. With very little help coming from the
    authorities in Tharsis City, Belle Song, her parents, and their friends from the neighboring
    farms join together to defeat the Raiders and protect their farms.
Identifiers: LCCN 2017002463 (print) | LCCN 2017008293 (ebook) |
    ISBN 9781496548207 (library binding) | ISBN 9781496548320 (eBook PDF)
Subjects: LCSH: Water-supply—Juvenile fiction. | Theft—Juvenile fiction. | Farm life—Juvenile
    fiction. | Citizens' associations--Juvenile fiction. | Science fiction. | Mars (Planet)—Juvenile
    fiction. | CYAC: Science fiction. | Water supply—Fiction. | Stealing—Fiction. | Farm life—
    Fiction. | Mars (Planet)—Fiction. | LCGFT: Science fiction.
Classification: LCC PZ7.1.C6447 Rai 2018 (print) | LCC PZ7.1.C6447 (ebook) |
    DDC 813.6 (Fic)—dc23
LC record available at https://lccn.loc.gov/2017002463

Editor: Aaron J. Sautter
Designer: Ted Williams
Production: Kathy McColley

Printed and bound in Canada.
010382F17

RAIDERS
WATER THIEVES OF MARS

BY A.L. COLLINS
ILLUSTRATED BY TOMISLAV TIKULIN

STONE ARCH BOOKS
a capstone imprint

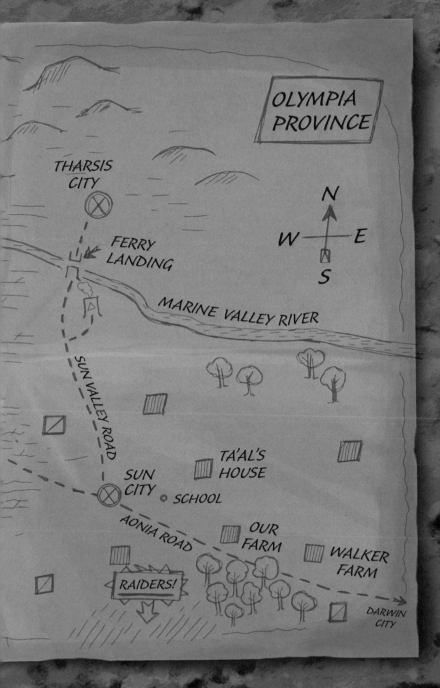

Belle Song

Twelve-year-old Belle can be headstrong and stubborn. Her curiosity and sense of adventure often get her into trouble. Still, she has a good heart and is passionate about fairness. She is fiercely loyal to her friends.

Yun and Zara Song

Belle's parents sometimes seem really strict. But Yun has a great sense of humor, which Belle both loves and is embarrassed by. Zara has a generous heart, which has taught Belle not to judge others too quickly.

Melody

Melody is an old model 3X Personal Home Helper android. She was given to Belle by her grandmother before she passed away. Melody is Belle's best friend and protector, and enjoys telling bad jokes to seem more human.

MAIN INHABITANTS

Lucas Walker

Lucas is Belle's neighbor and classmate. He is part Sulux and part human. Meeting new people is not easy for him. But once he knows someone, his adventurous side emerges. He is full of ideas, which sometimes gets him and his friends into trouble.

Ta'al

Ta'al and her family are Nabian, an ancient alien race from another star system. Born and raised on Mars, Ta'al is intelligent and curious. She enjoys exploring and adventure, and quickly becomes Belle's closest friend on Mars.

Raider

Raider is a hybrid wolf-dog. These animals were bred to be tame pets, but some of them became wild. After Raider is rescued by Belle, he becomes a faithful and protective companion.

It is the year 2335. Life on Earth is very difficult. Natural resources like trees, water, and oil are nearly gone. Many animal species have become extinct, and air pollution is causing widespread disease. More than 50 years ago, intelligent robots rose up to overthrow their human creators. After the Robot Rebellion ended, people were terrified of technology. Many Terrans, those who are from Earth, chose to avoid robots and returned to a more basic lifestyle. But a few families still use less advanced robots as companions for their children.

Many people moved to the Moon to begin a new life on Lunar Colony. But it is overcrowded and has limited resources. Other families chose to move to Mars instead. With the help of two alien races — the Sulux and the Nabians — the red planet was transformed to support life nearly two hundred years ago.

Hoping to find a better life, Yun and Zara Song and their daughter, Belle, left Earth and moved to Mars. There they began living as farmers. They work hard to grow crops and hybrid animals suitable for Mars.

Water is the most precious resource on Mars. Without it, nothing can survive. Unfortunately, some people would rather steal water from others than buy it legally. These Water Raiders pose a serious threat to every farmer trying to make a living on . . .

REDWORLD

CHAPTER ONE
SIGNS OF TROUBLE

"Fresh turken eggs, shoat milk, and cheese!" shouted twelve-year-old Belle.

The market at Sun City was especially crowded today. Belle was helping at her family's stall while her parents stocked up on supplies. All the farmers were getting ready for winter, buying everything they needed to keep them comfortable for the long, cold months ahead. Mars winters were harsh. Temperatures could plunge to 50 degrees below zero or more.

In four hours, Belle had sold all their produce. Only a few skeins of alpaca yarn were left on the table. Belle was proud that she'd helped her parents shear the alpacas on their farm. Belle's mom, Zara, had taught her how to spin the alpaca wool into yarn. Her mom had learned from her grandmother, who in turn had learned it from her grandmother. By market day, the Songs had a large collection of wool and yarn ready for sale.

"I suppose we can pack up now," Yun said as he returned with his own bundle of supplies. He seemed happy to see that sales had gone so well.

Zara dragged an enormous, colorful rug behind her. It was woven from shoat wool that had been dyed in various bright colors.

Zara exhaled and wiped her brow. "Please, let's go. I'm exhausted. I'll need help getting this rug onto the wagon. Yun insisted on buying it."

"It will come in handy during the cold nights," Melody chimed in. She was Belle's android and constant companion. With one heave, Melody lifted the rug with her strong arms and threw it into the back of their hover-wagon. She scanned the contents of the wagon, checking the items off a list that was displayed on the screen on her torso.

"It looks as if we are all set for winter," she announced. Her eyes glowed pink. Belle took this to mean that Melody was happy.

"Belle!"

Belle had one foot on the wagon's back step when she heard her name called. She turned around to see her Nabian friend, Ta'al, approaching.

"*Gyrvel*, my friend." Ta'al dipped her head and wove her hands in a delicate dancelike gesture. This was her people's way of greeting others.

"Where were you yesterday?" Belle said. "You weren't at school."

Ta'al dabbed a handkerchief on her nostrils, which were located on her ridged forehead. When they'd first met, it had taken Belle some time to get used to her alien friend's appearance. Ta'al looked human in some ways. She had two eyes, a mouth, ears, and humanoid body. But there were differences too. Her nostrils and ridges were the most obvious. And her black, plasticlike hair appeared to be one solid piece.

In spite of Ta'al's strange features, Belle thought her friend was beautiful. She especially liked Ta'al's large eyes that reflected the colors of her surroundings. Today, they were green and brownish orange, the colors of the marketplace.

"I caught a cold," Ta'al said. "I'm sad that I missed the end-of-year party. Was it good?"

Belle nodded. "But it wasn't any fun without you."

Ta'al laughed and prodded Belle's middle with her thick finger. "Silly girl," she said. "Now that I'm better, do you want to come over for *matekap* — a sleepover?"

Belle looked over at her parents, who had finished stacking their supplies in the wagon. They were busy checking that nothing was missing.

"That sounds like a lovely idea," Zara said, stepping out of the wagon and wiping her hands on her skirt. She smiled at Ta'al. "But I'd love to speak to your parents about it first, if you don't mind."

Ta'al pulled out a flat disc from somewhere under her many layers of clothing. She tapped on it several times, and then looked up. "They're on their way."

As they waited, Ta'al showed Belle her new communication device and how it worked using a code known only to Nabians.

Three large aliens, dressed like Ta'al in flowing layers of fabric, gracefully moved toward the Song family wagon. They looked like their feet barely touched the ground.

Yun descended from the wagon as they approached.

"Who's this, then?" he said, with his usual grin.

"Nabians have three parents," Ta'al explained. "The human equivalent of my mother is So'ark."

The tallest of the three Nabians stepped forward, with both hands outstretched. She took Zara's hand in one and Yun's in the other. "I am pleased to know you," she said. "This is He'ern, my first *elixian*. The closest word in your language is *equal*."

"He'ern's function is much like that of a father to humans," Ta'al said.

He'ern greeted them all in the same way. Then he introduced Fa'erz, their third *elixian*.

"Without Fa'erz, I would not exist," Ta'al said. "To my knowledge, humans don't have an equivalent to the role Fa'erz plays in our family."

Belle had so many questions, but thought it best to keep them to herself. She didn't want to be rude. And she definitely wanted to do a sleepover. She hadn't had a sleepover since moving to Mars.

"We'll have so much fun," Ta'al whispered to Belle as their parents talked. "I have some new gadgets that I can't wait to show you."

Before Belle could ask about the gadgets, Lucas Walker came running up to them. Lucas was in the same class as the girls, and his family's farm neighbored the Songs' land.

He and Belle had become good friends in the last months, but for some unknown reason, he didn't like Ta'al. His parents, Myra and Paddy, followed closely behind Lucas.

"Come on, neighbor," Paddy said to Yun, chuckling. "Time to get going." But then he stopped very suddenly. He stared at the Nabians. "Having some trouble, Yun?"

"Not at all," Yun said, puzzled.

"Have you met Ta'al's parents?" Belle asked.

Lucas scowled at Ta'al, the same way he'd scowled at Belle when they'd first met. Back then he explained he'd been shy about meeting new people. But he'd known Ta'al longer than Belle. Yet, he never talked to Ta'al in school.

Belle didn't expect him to behave differently now. It was his parents' reaction that surprised Belle the most. Grown ups were supposed to have better manners. But Myra and Paddy ignored Ta'al's parents too!

For a long moment, no one spoke. The adults stared at the ground or the wagon. It was extremely awkward.

"We're ready to go as soon as you are, Paddy." Zara finally broke the silence. "It was so nice to meet you, So'ark. I hope we can set up a play date soon."

"Mom!" Belle cried. "I'm too old for *play dates*. It's a sleepover. A mat . . . a *matekap*. Why can't I go tonight?"

Zara gave Belle a stern look. "You can't go tonight. We have to get home and unload the wagon before dark. We can talk about it later."

"It's okay Belle, we can plan another time. Until then, we can work on your pronunciation." Ta'al smiled.

Ta'al's family bowed their heads and walked on past the Song's wagon without another word. Ta'al turned to wave, and Belle waved back.

Myra Walker shook her head. As soon as Ta'al's family was out of sight she turned to Zara. "Are you sure you want Belle socializing with a Nabian?" she asked.

"Ta'al is my friend!" Belle was surprised at how loud her outburst was. She bit her lip.

Paddy put his arm around Yun. "It's just best not to," he said, speaking softly as if he were telling Yun a secret. "You know, for the safety of your family."

Yun nodded without speaking.

Paddy patted him on the back. "Good man," he said. "Let's be off then."

In the wagon, Belle was troubled during the ride home.

"Why don't the Walkers like Ta'al's family?" she asked her mom, who was programming knitting patterns into an old household robot.

"I have found some historical archives," Melody said. "They might explain the tension between the Martians, the Sulux, and the Nabians."

"Tension?" Belle said. "But I remember reading that Sulux and Nabians came from the same planetary system."

"That is correct," Melody said.

"Yes, one system over from Earth's solar system," Zara added. "I remember you telling me that."

"So they were neighbors," Belle said. "Why would an alien species hate their neighbors?" Belle asked. "I'm an alien here too, since I was born on Earth. Does someone hate me for being Terran?"

"Of course not," Zara said. "We don't hate each other for where we're from. That's primitive."

"But that's what's happening here," Belle said. "I just want to know why."

"Perhaps some studying will help you discover the answers you seek," Melody said. Sometimes she sounded like an ancient professor. But this time she might just be right.

Belle settled down to read the documents that appeared on Melody's chest display. She was quite absorbed in the history of Mars when she was jolted out of her seat.

"What was that?" she cried, regaining her balance.

Loki, their horsel, whinnied and stopped pulling the hover-wagon. He sounded scared. Then Belle heard her dad yell. She peeked her head out the front by the bench seat where Yun sat.

They were at their farm gate. Beyond it, Belle saw that all their animals were loose and running around. Alpacas and shoats roamed the front yard. Meanwhile, turkens pecked and scratched in Zara's little vegetable patch.

"Did we have a power outage?" Zara asked as she got down to open the gate.

"Maybe. But we have backup power," Yun said, guiding Loki through the gate.

As Melody began chasing the fowl back into the big barn, Belle ran to one of the corrals. "Some of the corral posts have been damaged," she said. "Could the alpacas have done that?"

Yun examined the posts. He was quiet for a long time. Suddenly he ran to the back of the house. Belle followed while Zara led Loki to the stables.

"Good. The water tank is safe," Yun said, as Belle reached him. He scratched his head. "But it looks like someone made this mess on purpose."

"Who would do that?" Belle couldn't believe it. They were only gone for the day.

Sol 110/Autumn, Mars Cycle 105

Someone wrecked our fences and let the animals loose. Dad thinks it could be water raiders. I don't know who did it, but it was scary. I'm so glad we weren't home and that our security system held the intruders off. But why did they have to go and release all the animals?

I'm too scared to sleep. I did more research on the Nabians and Sulux instead. This is what I learned:

1. They're both from planets in the same binary solar system — that means they have two suns.
2. They both came to Earth for a first contact conference when the Terrans achieved interstellar flight.
3. Nabians are an ancient race. They're much older than the Sulux. They may even be related. But don't ever say that to them.
4. Nabians claim that they were on Mars long before Terrans. They resent the Sulux for sharing their terraforming technology.
5. Sulux think the Nabians are jealous of their friendship with Martian humans.

Basically, they've hated each other for years. And there's no convincing either side to be nice to the other. But I don't understand why humans should care. Why should we treat Nabians like they're the bad guys?

CHAPTER TWO
:HOME DEFENSES:

The following evening, Belle sat quietly at the dining table, listening as her dad spoke to the Olympian authorities. It had taken him all day to reach them on the holo-vid. The authorities enforced the law for the entire region in the shadow of the enormous volcano, Mount Olympus. They operated out of Tharsis City, Olympia's capital, on the other side of the Marine Valley River.

"If your tank is intact and nothing was stolen, there isn't much I can do." The holo-vid of the man's head floated above the dining table like an eerie balloon. He wasn't even looking at his camera.

The hologram also lit up Yun's face, making him look angry. "Then what am I supposed to do? The raiders will return. I'm sure they were just testing our defenses."

"Like I said, there's nothing —"

"— you can do," Yun interrupted. "I got that. You might as well say I should put up a sign inviting them to just take my water."

The man finally looked up. He had circles under his eyes. Belle wondered if a lot of people complained to him every day. He slowly shook his head. "All I can say is, some other communities have formed their own, sort of, watchdog groups. We don't condone violence, of course. People can't just take the law into their own hands. But banding together to keep these raiders out has worked in the past."

The man continued, "It helps to build morale too. I wouldn't worry too much. These raids won't last long. Raiders tend to get desperate right before winter sets in."

The screen fizzled out and the holo-vid faded back into the computer. Yun slammed his fists on the table, making Belle jump.

"I'm sorry, Belle," he said when he saw how scared she was. "It's just so frustrating."

Belle put a hand on her dad's shoulder. "I think it's a good idea to have a team of neighbors looking out for each other. I'd be happy to get Lucas and the other kids together to see what we can do."

Yun smiled at her. "You're very thoughtful. But please don't worry too much. This is an adult problem. Let the adults handle it."

Belle hated being told that she was too young to be helpful. Her parents didn't know how good her inventions were. She could help to protect their home just as well as they could.

"It's time for bed," Zara said.

"But it's barely sunset," Belle argued.

"You have to get up early for school tomorrow," Zara replied. "We don't want to keep Lucas waiting for you." Sun City school met only twice a week, and on those days, Belle walked to school with Lucas.

"Besides," her mom continued, "we need to give Dad some space to figure things out. Now, off to bed with you."

Belle knew this was an argument she couldn't win. So she and Melody headed to her room.

"I can't sleep this early," Belle whined to Melody.

"We could think up some new jokes," Melody said. "I will start. What did one ocean say to the other ocean?"

"I'm not in the mood for jokes," Belle snapped. Then she felt bad for being so rude to her friend. Melody was only trying to cheer her up. "What did the ocean say?" she asked.

"Nothing," Melody replied. "It just waved."

Belle rolled her eyes and shook her head. That was bad. "No more. Please."

"Then perhaps you should work on your science project?" The android suggested. Belle's class had been divided into teams of two for the upcoming science fair. She and Lucas had been researching methods for growing turken fowl bigger and faster. They were supposed to make their final presentation on their project before the school year ended. The top two projects from the whole school would be chosen to present their findings at the Olympia Science Fair in Tharsis City the next summer.

Melody projected Belle's last homework entry onto the wall. Belle's turken chicks were growing very well eating the new mixture of food she and Lucas had created.

An hour later Belle put away her datapad. "I can't do any more until Lucas does his part," she said. "We're meeting tomorrow after school anyway. We'll do it together then."

Belle couldn't stop thinking about the raiders. She couldn't help worrying, no matter what her dad said. "I think we should make more Petripuffs."

Belle's Petripuffs were her pride and joy. She'd spent a lot of time working on perfecting them. She'd won first prize with them at her last science fair on Earth. Her parents had been too busy with work to see her receive her award, which made her sad. But she was still very proud of herself.

Now her Petripuffs had become more than just a science fair project. They were very useful in the Wild West of Mars. The small palm-sized balls broke open when they hit a target. They then released a powder that could paralyze anyone who breathed it in. The effect only lasted about thirty seconds. But in a dangerous situation, that time could mean the difference between getting hurt and escaping unharmed.

Melody moved to the cabinet where Belle kept the special ingredients for her puffs. It was kept locked because one ingredient, the most important one, was unstable, and required careful handling.

"You have already put several puffs in the barn, in case the wolves return," Melody said, as she activated the locking mechanism. There was a quiet click as it unlocked.

"True, but we'll need more," Belle said. "Especially now that we also have to deal with raiders."

"We're running low on PF-51," Belle said as she completed her second puff. "And the gel stuff that binds it all together."

Melody's turned to face Belle. Her mouth glowed yellow. This was Melody's sarcastic smile. "Gel stuff? How scientific of you."

Melody was good at sarcasm.

"You know what I mean."

"I will add the 'stuff' to my list," Melody said, still glowing. "It is late now. Time for bed."

As Belle lay in bed, she watched the stars twinkle outside her window. "The universe is so big," she said with a sigh.

"That is a given," Melody said, as she plugged herself into her charging port. "Your point being?"

"Nothing," Belle said. "I was just thinking how there must be millions of aliens out there. There must be all different kinds. Some more different than others."

"Another given." Melody's charger hummed quietly.

"Do you think they all hate each other?" Belle asked.

"That would seem unlikely," Melody replied. "I would need more specific information."

Belle didn't say anything.

"But if you are referring to the Sulux and the Nabians," Melody said, lowering her volume, "their fight goes back many generations. Prejudice is seen in their every encounter."

"But their problems shouldn't affect us kids or be brought into our classroom," Belle argued. "Ta'al is a good person, and a great friend. She deserves a chance to fit in. We should all learn to work together — not let old issues separate us."

"It will take more than the opinion of one little girl to bring them together in friendship," Melody responded.

Belle yawned. "I'm not a little girl. And I believe a person can change the world . . . if she cares enough." She rolled over and shut her eyes.

"Well quoted, my young friend." Melody's eyes glowed bright pink for a second, just before she powered down for the night.

Sol 112/Autumn, Mars Cycle 105, early morning

I was woken by the weirdest dream last night. I was a Nabian and Lucas was chasing after me. His whole family was trying to catch me. I didn't know why, but I was afraid. I couldn't shake the fear, so I decided to just get up early.

Melody's still charging. No one is awake. But outside, I hear the howl of wolves. I hope they don't come back. Just the sound of their howls is enough to give me goosebumps.

I must find a way to get Lucas to see how good a person Ta'al is. We should all be friends.

CHAPTER THREE
STANDING UP FOR A FRIEND

After Belle and Lucas had been paired up for the science fair project, the walk to school became a time to discuss their progress. But once they reached school, Lucas usually ignored both Belle and Ta'al.

Belle was determined to change that. Somehow.

"It looks like the fifty percent micro-algae combination works the best so far," Lucas said. As they walked and talked, he kept his eyes on his datapad, which showed their project results. "We're ready for our presentation today."

"If you don't look up occasionally, you will trip over something," Melody said. The android had decided to walk with them to school today. Belle suspected it was because of the previous incident with the raiders.

Lucas looked at Melody. "I'll never get used to talking to an android like it was another person."

"She's not an 'it,'" Belle reminded him again. "There's no reason to be afraid of her."

Lucas put the report away, sliding his datapad into his backpack. "Everyone's afraid of intelligent androids. I watched all the old news holo-vids of the fight between robots and people on Earth. It was scary."

"That was years ago, before our parents were even born," Belle said. "And Melody would never harm anyone."

Lucas shrugged. "She'd better not."

"I am a Personal Home Helper," Melody said, looking directly at Lucas. "I am not designed to hurt humans."

Lucas didn't reply.

As soon as the school building came into view, Lucas looked to the right and then ran on ahead. From the path to Belle's right, Ta'al approached, seeming to glide along as if she traveled above the ground. Belle stared at Ta'al's tiny feet as they peeked out from under her long cloak. Belle couldn't work out exactly how Ta'al could move with such gracefulness. It was one difference she'd noticed between the Nabians and the Sulux. Lucas wasn't nearly as graceful as Ta'al.

"Sorry I interrupted your talk with Lucas," she said. She was wearing layers of light-colored fabric that reminded Belle of fairy wings. Each layer looked fragile and shiny in the autumn morning sun.

"It wasn't you," Belle said, looking over at her android. "He still gets a little freaked out by Melody."

Ta'al waved to Melody, who greeted her in Ta'al's own language.

"That's incredible," Ta'al said. "You have perfect pronunciation."

"*Sia-mi* — thank you," Melody said. "I do my best."

Belle beamed. Her android *was* the best.

"I'll leave you now," Melody said as they reached the school gate. "I will meet you here after school."

"See you then," Belle said, grabbing Ta'al's hand. Together they ran to the gray block building that held the town's school, library, community center, and medical facility.

● ● ● ·

Lucas and Belle's project presentation went very well. Lucas had made all kinds of charts, using the data that Belle had gathered. They spoke with confidence as they explained how their new food formula made turken chicks grow fifty percent bigger in half the usual time.

Ms. Polley was impressed.

Belle was so pleased that she barely paid attention to the next report by Trina and Pavish. Every project had to be about agriculture, which was the rule for the science fair. Agriculture didn't interest Belle very much. She had to admit, though, that she was starting to like the turkens. She remembered when she first got them as a gift from Lucas' mom. She hated how they smelled and their sharp claws. Now they were easy to handle and seemed to smell less.

The last students to present their project were Brill and Ta'al. Brill rushed up to the front with his datapad and opened up a holo-file. Everyone could see it was full of notes. Ta'al stayed at her desk.

"Are you the only one presenting?" Ms. Polley asked.

Brill pointed at Ta'al. "She won't help with the project, so I did it myself."

Everyone looked at Ta'al, who examined her fingers.

Belle leaned over and whispered. "What's wrong? Was he mean to you?"

Ta'al only blinked without looking up.

"Ta'al," Ms. Polley said, in a tone everyone knew meant she was in trouble. "Is this true? Are you being uncooperative?"

Ta'al didn't respond.

"Answer me, Ta'al," Ms. Polley said more firmly.

"Come on," Belle whispered again. "You should tell her the truth."

"Can't ever expect a Nabian to do their part," Lucas mumbled. The others snorted.

"That's really rude," Belle snapped. "You don't even know the whole story."

Lucas stood up. "You can't trust Nabians. They're just a bunch of lazy raiders."

Belle smacked her hand on her desk so hard that her datapad screen fizzled. "You take that back, Lucas Walker!"

"I will not!" he yelled. "Everyone knows that the raiders are Nabians. They want to rule Mars. But they can't, so they make it hard for the rest of us to live here. And they're jealous of the Sulux."

The other kids murmured "yeah" and nodded. Belle could feel her blood pressure rise, making her face hot. She couldn't believe what Lucas was saying. In all her research, there was no hint that the Nabians ever tried to rule Mars.

"Nabians are a peaceful race," Belle said, trying hard not to shout. "Just read their history."

"I don't care about their history," he said. "It's what they're doing now that's causing problems for everyone."

"You're wrong, Lucas!" Belle shouted. "That's illogical and ignorant."

"That's enough, Lucas . . . and Belle," Ms. Polley said. But it was too late. So many nasty things had been said.

In all of the ruckus, no one saw that Ta'al was now standing. Her eyes were wide and full of rage.

"Ms. Polley," she said. Her voice was steady, but Belle could sense the anger behind her words. "I gave Brill many ideas, good ideas, for projects. But he refused to listen — *si ner toh khan*! He chose to conduct the simplest experiment. There was nothing I could do to make him cooperate."

"Her ideas weren't science," Brill protested. "They were more like magical hocus pocus — weird alien stuff."

"I'd think you'd jump at the chance to learn about alien science. Something new that we don't know anything about," Belle said.

Ms. Polley clapped her hands loudly. The whole class stopped and turned to look at her. She sighed and pushed her curly, black hair away from her face. The red

rings around her irises — the rings that all Martian-born humans had — glowed like fire. The class watched her in silence for several long minutes.

"Fine," she finally said. "Brill, you can complete your own project. Maybe pair up with your younger brother. Fourth graders are eligible to enter the fair too." She moved around her desk and sat down. "Ta'al, if you want to compete in the Olympian Science Fair, you'll need a partner. As there are no other Nabians in this school, I don't know how to help you. Is there anyone you're willing to work with?"

Ta'al didn't move. Only her eyes flickered over to Belle for a second.

Fed up with all the fighting, Belle piped up. "I'll work with her, Ms. Polley."

"You can't," Lucas said. "You're my partner."

"I can do two projects," Belle said. "Winter will be so boring anyway, and Ta'al and I can work remotely." She looked over at Ta'al, who gave Belle a slight nod. "If that's okay with you, Ms. Polley."

Ms. Polley threw her hands in the air. "If you think you can handle it, Isabelle Song, you're welcome to enter two projects." Then she exhaled loudly, stood up, and continued with the day's subjects.

At the end of the school day, Lucas ran off toward home with Brill, leaving Belle alone to wait for Melody. Ta'al, who had to stay behind to speak to Ms. Polley, caught up to Belle at the school gate.

"Melody's late," Belle said. "That's not like her."

"She'll be here soon," Ta'al said. "Why don't we meet her on the path?"

The girls walked until they reached the fork in the path that Ta'al took to get home. There was no Melody in sight.

"I'll walk with you," Ta'al offered.

"But it's too far from your home."

"I'll ask Fa'erz to come get me later. We can talk about our science project."

Belle listened intently as Ta'al shared her ideas. They were so different and interesting that Belle was excited to be working with her. She didn't even notice the time pass as they walked along.

Abruptly, Ta'al stopped talking.

"What is it?" Belle asked.

Ta'al pointed ahead. As Belle turned to look, she gasped. There in front of the girls was the Song farm. And it was on fire!

CHAPTER FOUR

ATTACKED!

Belle stood frozen to the ground. Her hands gripped the farm gate so hard that her fingers had gone white. Black smoke rose from behind the above-ground portion of their home. The air was filled with ash, making it hard to breathe. Loud pops and crackles were mixed with the shrieking of animals. The sight of it all scared Belle too much to move.

"I'll call for firebots," Ta'al said. Her calm voice helped Belle to begin breathing again.

"My parents!" Belle shoved open the gate and ran. As she reached the house, she saw Melody leaning over her dad's body. He wasn't moving.

"Is he . . . ?" She didn't dare finish the question.

"He is unconscious," Melody said, as if it were an interesting factoid. "He will be fine. I am taking him into the house." Belle was grateful for Melody's lack of emotion. If she said Yun wasn't in danger, then he'd be all right.

Belle watched as Melody lifted her dad up in her mechanical arms and carried him toward their home. Then she headed to the back area behind the house. With each step, she felt the heat of the blaze. She couldn't believe her eyes. The field behind the house was on fire. Flames rose almost as high as the barn. Zara was in one corner of the field. She and one farmbot were trying to put out the fire with extinguishers. Their efforts barely made a difference.

"Firebots are on their way," Belle called to her mom. "What happened?"

Zara's face was full of soot and ash, as were her hands. She put down the extinguisher, then ran over to Belle and hugged her tight. Belle could feel her mom's ragged breathing and knew she was trying not to cry.

"It'll be all right," Zara said over and over again.

"But how did this happen?" asked Belle.

"Raiders . . ." She didn't have to say more.

Belle began to cry. It wasn't until she heard the hum of drones overhead that she stopped.

"We should get out of the way," Zara said, waving the farm droids away.

Five firefighting drones hovered over the area where the water tank was buried. White pebbles rained down from above. When they hit the ground, they began expanding into white foam. Within minutes the fire was out. Zara stood bent over, with her hands on her knees, panting.

"Melody took dad inside the house," Belle said, her voice trembling. Seeing her mom like this scared her.

Zara straightened. She looked as if she'd forgotten all about Yun. "He was stunned when he went after them. But there were too many, and they had weapons." She marched back toward the house with Belle running after her. "We should report this. We need to get Protectors out here immediately."

As they reached the house, Myra Walker and Lucas came running up the driveway.

"We saw the smoke," Myra said. "How bad is it?"

Zara told Myra the whole story. They'd been out in the fields harvesting when they heard the rumble of engines. Two vehicles each carrying half a dozen raiders crashed through their back fences, right where the water tank was. Within seconds, they were pumping out water. Yun had gone to get his sonic blaster as Melody and Zara approached the raiders.

"We used some of your puffs, Belle," her mom said.

"You know about my Petripuffs?"

"Melody told us, so we threw a few at the Raiders," she said. "It kept them occupied long enough for your dad to get his blaster. Then he chased them off. But as they left, one of them threw some kind of explosive device at the tank. There was a terrible explosion, and then the fire."

Zara had her hand on her chest. She was breathing fast.

"All is well now," Myra said, draping an arm over Zara. "Let's go inside and report it. Children, you should all come in as well. Get out of the firebots' way as they finish their work."

Lucas followed his mom without a word. Belle turned around to look for Ta'al. She'd forgotten all about her, but it was Ta'al that had saved them, really. She had called for the firebot drones. Belle saw Ta'al standing by the farm gate. She looked unsure of what to do.

"Come inside with me," Belle cried, waving to her friend.

Ta'al ran over. Her eyes were wet with tears and reflected the black smoke of the fire. Belle gave her a hug.

"Thank you so much," Belle said.

● ● ● ●

Yun was lying unconscious in his bed when Belle went in to see him. His face was covered in soot, just like Zara's. Melody hovered over him, scanning him from head to toe.

"He should wake up soon," she said. "He has no permanent damage."

In a moment Yun blinked his eyes open. Belle held his hand in hers. She fought back the tears. She wanted to be brave for her dad. When he saw her, he smiled.

"That was quite an experience," he said. "I've never been stunned before." He pushed himself to a sitting position, but held his hand to his head. "And I don't think I ever want to be stunned again." He chuckled weakly.

"Why are you laughing?" Belle asked.

"What else can I do?" He rubbed his head. "If I think about what we've lost, I might cry like a small child. And what good would that do?"

He ruffled the top of Belle's head, making her feel like that small child. It annoyed her when he did and said things that sounded like kids were weak. But she didn't correct him. He had earned a pass to express his old-fashioned ideas. Just this once.

In the kitchen, Zara was already talking to the authorities. When she saw Yun, she insisted he sit back down again.

"They're sending a Protector out today," she said, signing off the holo-vid.

"One Protector?" he said. "Is that enough?"

"Have you ever met a Protector?" Myra said. She was busy making tea for everyone. "They do the work of ten humans combined. Or Sulux."

"Are you all right?" Lucas said to Belle, when she joined her friends in the living room.

Belle patted Ta'al on the shoulder. "I am, thanks to Ta'al's cool-headedness."

Ta'al's face went purple. She almost matched Lucas. "I just did what anyone else would have done."

Lucas looked at Ta'al in a way Belle had never seen before. It was almost a smile. "Well, I'm glad you were there to help," he said. "Belle, I should've walked you home. I'm sorry I was mad at you."

Belle couldn't believe her ears. Lucas was being nice to both of them! She leaned in closer to her two friends.

"We need to come up with a plan to stop these raiders," she whispered. Her parents wouldn't approve, but she couldn't sit back and be helpless. "Will you help me?"

Ta'al's eyes widened. Lucas' eyes narrowed.

"Come on, Lucas," Belle said. "You don't really believe Ta'al's family is involved in the raids, do you?"

"Not them, specifically," he said, looking down at his hands. "But, you know, the rumors about Nabians —"

The doorbell rang. Belle ran to answer it before she could answer Lucas. She was surprised to see Paddy Walker at the door, talking respectfully to So'ark, He'ern, and Fa'erz. He gestured for Ta'al's parents to enter first.

After checking to see if Yun and the others were okay, Paddy coughed to get everyone's attention.

"I've called for a meeting of all seven of the neighboring farm families," he said importantly. "Everyone has agreed to be at our house tomorrow night." Paddy nodded to So'ark. His face was redder than Belle had ever seen. "It's about time we stand up to these monsters once and for all."

Belle went over to her friends.

"Rumors about the Nabians need to be proven before I'll believe them," she whispered. "In the meantime, we should work together to stop the raids. Kids too, not just adults. Agreed?"

Both Ta'al and Lucas looked up at their parents, then back at Belle. They nodded. Belle's heart skipped a beat. This was her chance to get back at the raiders for what they had done to her family and her home.

Sol 113/Autumn, Mars Cycle 105, early morning

I have to come up with a plan to help fight the raiders. I've got my Petripuffs, and I can teach my friends how to make them. But they're not enough. We need other defenses too. I'm hoping there will be other kids at the farmers' meeting tonight, and we'll be able to come up with more inventions.

The Protector arrived just after midnight, but my parents wouldn't let me go out to watch the inspection of the damage. So I'm stuck in my room. They said I would get in the way. How rude! I was a witness too. But my parents wouldn't listen.

Well, I refuse to sit back and let others protect us. This is my home too. I also need to do more research. I can't believe the Nabians would have anything to do with the raiders. Everything I've read tells me they're a peaceful people. Why does everyone believe they're bad?

CHAPTER FIVE

NEIGHBORS UNITED

The next morning the shiny silver and black Protector stood in the Walkers' living room as neighbor after neighbor fired questions at it. Belle hadn't taken her eyes off the android. It was the biggest one she'd ever seen.

This Protector was humanoid in shape, like Melody. But it was three times bigger than her. It had all kinds of gadgets attached to its body. Belle was sure it probably had several hidden weapons and instruments in its body as well.

It had one roaming red eye that seemed to constantly scan its surroundings. This android was definitely intelligent. And no one seemed to mind it being in the house. How were Martians not afraid of these huge androids, yet still afraid of an old robot like Melody?

"When will the authorities start to care about the farmers?" asked Mr. Park, one of the oldest neighbors. "Without us, people in the cities would have no food."

"We need real assistance out here, especially as winter approaches," Paddy added.

The Protector didn't answer their questions. It just kept repeating, "Investigations are underway. We are close to finding the criminals."

"Can you share the results of your investigations?" Yun said.

"That information is classified." The red eye blinked over at Belle and the other kids sitting in the corner.

One farmer, who had been silent for most of the meeting, stood up. He pointed to So'ark, He'ern, and Fa'erz, who had also come for the meeting. "Before we go on, how do we know you lot aren't here to spy on us? You might go telling the raiders what actions we're going to take."

Yun put a hand on his shoulder. "Now, Harry, let's not turn on each other. We're all in this together."

"And there's no evidence that the Nabians are even involved in the raids," Zara said. "They're just rumors, spread by ignorant, frightened people." She went to sit with So'ark.

"So how come they've never been raided then?" Harry said. "And I've heard that some Nabians around here have gone missing 'cuz they've joined the raider gangs. Isn't that enough to make anyone suspicious?"

He'ern stood up, his hands clasped tightly in front of his body. He spoke in deliberate, measured tones. "The missing Nabians have been reported to the authorities. Their families are worried for their safety. And we have a security system that is far beyond your technology. I hardly think that is evidence of our involvement with the enemy."

"Yun is right," Paddy said, surprising everyone. "Nothing will get done if we argue among ourselves. We're in this together. Let's get on with this meeting, shall we?"

Harry sat back down, grumbling.

"So, Protector, tell us what exactly the authorities will do to help us," Yun said. "Please be specific."

The Protector repeated the stories of how other farms had formed neighborhood patrols. They used farmbots to keep watch at night. Neighbors also kept an eye on each other's farms when families were traveling. Each suggestion was greeted with complaints that it wasn't enough.

"The raiders are getting more violent," Mr. Park said. "Didn't you see the damage done to the Song farm?"

"Investigations are underway —"

"Yeah, yeah, we get it. 'You are close to finding them.'" Paddy rubbed his face with both hands, as if he was trying to keep himself awake.

The farmers tried to pry suggestions out of the Protector for the next hour. When they got no satisfactory answers, they shook their heads. They had to accept the fact that they'd be on their own to stop the raiders.

"We cannot condone violence," the Protector said.

"But if you won't help us, we'll have no choice." Yun walked right up to the giant android. "You've given us no guarantee that anything will be done."

The Protector repeated his usual line again.

Yun threw his hands up. "I guess we're on our own."

"Can't you do something, Melody?" Belle whispered to her android.

Melody moved over to the Protector while the neighbors were busy talking. As they made plans to patrol the farms, Belle kept her eyes on Melody as she communicated with the Protector.

Just as the schedule was set for the farmbots to patrol the farm borders, the Protector spoke up. Its deep voice vibrated through the underground home, and right through Belle's body.

"I will authorize five drones to fly regular routes over the farms in the Sun City area," the Protector said. "They will patrol all day and night, until the first day of winter. Is that acceptable?"

No one said a word in response. They were all too shocked to speak.

"Well, it's a start," Paddy said eventually. He walked up and shook the Protector's hand. "If you'd said that in the beginning, you'd have saved us all a lot of trouble."

Belle patted Melody on the back. "Well done," she said with a grin.

"I simply reminded him of his duty to serve and protect," Melody said. "And I highlighted some Protector actions taken in Utopia, when they had similar troubles. I find that previous practices make for a strong case."

"Well, now it's our turn," Belle said.

Belle nodded to Lucas, who gestured for the kids to follow him to his room. Her classmates and two younger kids had come with their parents that night. They'd all agreed to join Belle in her scheme.

Belle stood in front of the group with a holo-document displayed on Lucas' bedroom wall and a digital pen in her hand. "First, we need to figure out what weapons we can use against the raiders. We need something that won't get us in trouble with our parents," she said. Everyone looked at her worriedly. "Don't worry. We'll be defending our homes, not going on the attack. Now let's think."

There was a collective sigh of relief. Then Ta'al spoke up.

"I've built a sonic disrupter device. It creates a loud, high-pitched sound," she said. "It will disable someone instantly, without permanent damage."

"But won't that hurt the user's ears too?" Lucas asked, looking skeptical.

Ta'al pulled something out of her pocket. "These are auditory shields."

Belle squinted at the rubbery things. "Ear plugs?"

"I suppose you could call them that." Ta'al demonstrated by shoving them into her ears and yelling, "If you wear them, you are protected from my disrupter!" That was the loudest Belle had ever heard her speak. She laughed. Ta'al laughed too, and soon everyone was chuckling.

Lucas shared his idea for a slingshot that shot pellets of a gel-like substance. "As soon as it hits the target, the gel expands to cover a large area in sticky goo. It's awesome!"

"I like that you use ingredients that can be found at home," Belle said. "We have to be careful not to spend

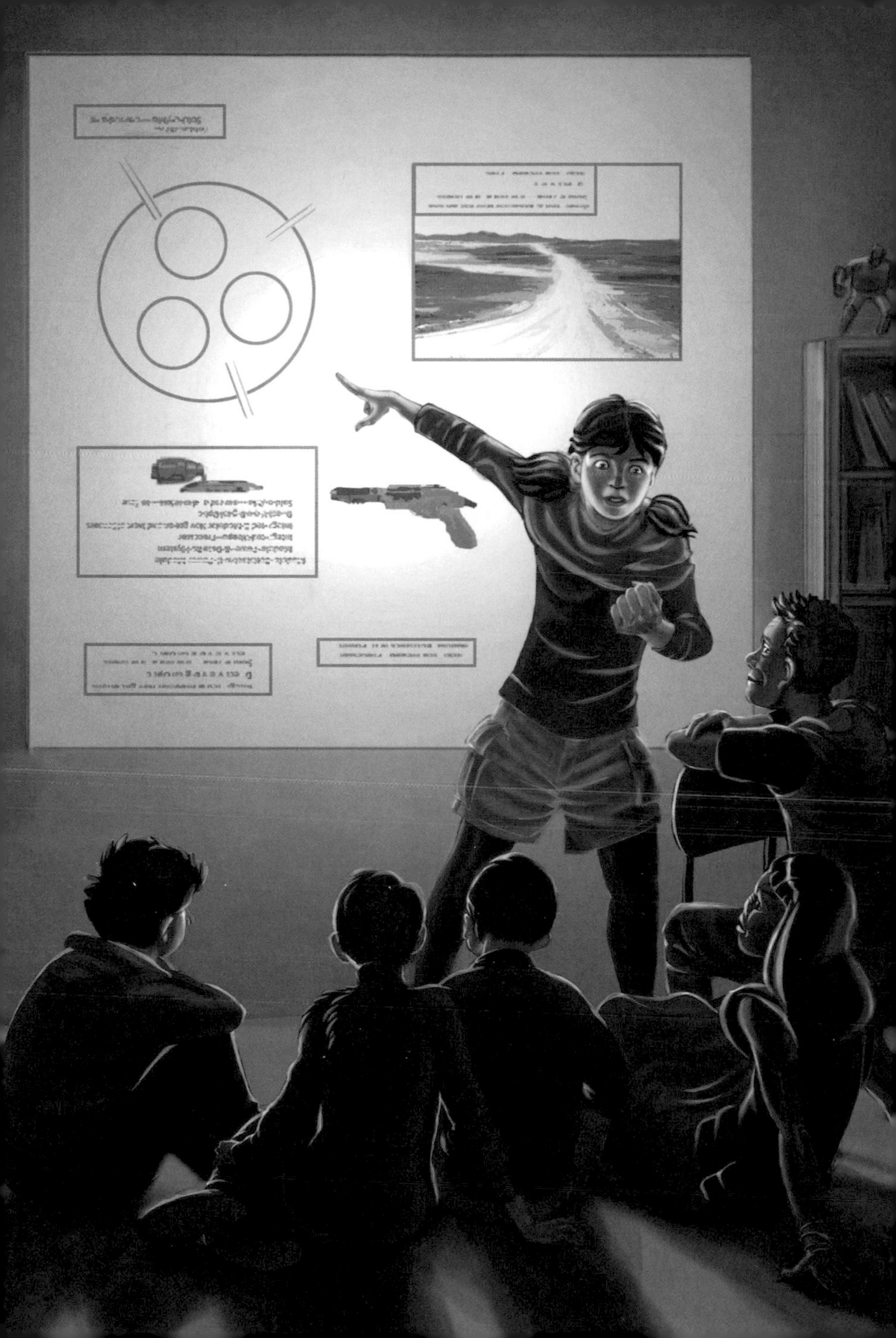

money. It'll make our parents suspicious." Even as she said it, she knew she'd have to pay for the PF-51 that Melody had ordered. It was the one ingredient for her puffs that couldn't be found at home.

Trina and Pavish thought of booby-trapping their water tanks with tripwires that set off a blaring alarm. Brill suggested filling his paintball pellets with itching powder. The two youngest kids wanted to fill bags with alpaca manure and set them around the water tanks. If the raiders stepped in them, it would make them stink.

Belle applauded everyone's ideas. "Great! We'll spend tomorrow making as many of our weapons as possible. Then we'll meet in my barn to share them. Deal?"

"Deal!" Everyone clapped.

● ● ● ●

As the Song family walked home that night Melody lit the way with her brightly shining eyes. Belle skipped along the path ahead of her parents.

"You seem happy tonight," Yun remarked.

Zara stopped in her tracks. "Wait. What have you got up your sleeve, Belle? I know you."

"What are you thinking, Belle?" Yun said.

"Nothing," Belle said, trying her best to look innocent.

Yun put his hands on Belle's shoulders. Somewhere in the distance two scavenger birds cawed at each other.

"Listen to me," Yun said sternly. "Raiders are no joke. They're vicious. Trust me, I know from personal experience. I don't want you getting involved and putting yourself or your friends in danger. Do you hear me?"

Belle nodded, avoiding her dad's eyes.

"Promise me you won't do anything stupid, Isabelle," he said.

"I promise." Belle bit her lip in frustration. She thought her plan was anything but stupid. In fact, it was brilliant.

Sol 113/Autumn, Mars Cycle 105, evening

Tonight the other kids and I put together a list of weapons we can use to defend our farms. If we all share what we have, we can be prepared for another raid. I believe we kids can help fight back against the raiders. After all, these are our homes too!

On another note, I think I'm making progress on getting Lucas to be friends with Ta'al. He actually spoke to her at his house. It's a first step.

CHAPTER SIX
AN UNEXPECTED GUEST

The next morning Belle jumped out of bed, devoured her breakfast, and ran outside before her mom could ask what was up. She walked past the charred backyard that looked like a giant black and grey pancake. Belle was thankful that at least the barn had been spared from the fire.

"I can prep the puffs ahead of time," she said to Melody, who met her by the barn. "Then when the PF-51 arrives, all we have to do is the final assembly."

"But first, you must complete your homework assignment," Melody reminded her.

For the first half of the morning, Belle measured and weighed her turkens, and then recorded all the information in her datapad. The birds eating the special diet were growing fast. Their big, brown feathers were silky and strong. Their red wattles were beginning to grow, and they were loud and enthusiastic when it came to feeding time.

"Compared to the other birds eating regular feed," Belle said, shutting off her datapad, "these are like super-chicks."

"Your project appears to be doing well. You have a good chance to represent your school in Tharsis City next summer." Melody leaned over the pens, taking holo-images of each turken for Belle's charts. The android's eyes glowed a deep pink. Melody was proud of Belle's work.

"I hope so," Belle said. "But there's also my other project with Ta'al. I wonder what we'll be doing?"

"Nabians are more advanced than Sulux and humans," Melody said. "I am curious why they bother with a planet like Mars. We are quite far behind them, technologically."

"Well, I can't wait to find out what ideas Ta'al has," Belle said. "Now, on to making more Petripuffs."

Melody assisted as Belle worked to assemble the delicate weapons. Belle began by making a gel-like substance, mixing it together with her hands. Then Melody used a special pump attached to her arm to gently blow the gel into small thin-skinned bubbles. Three gel bubbles would fit in each Petripuff. Belle injected ground pebble dust into one set of bubbles. She had collected a lot of pebbles and ground them into dust. Melody filled another set of bubbles with a pressurized gas. The third set of bubbles would be filled with PF-51. The chemical would create a paralyzing gas when mixed with the other two ingredients. Since the PF-51 hadn't arrived yet, Melody placed the empty bubbles in trays. They glistened in the bright sunlight that shone through the open barn doors.

They worked quietly, concentrating on the process. As Melody reached out to place a delicate bubble onto a tray, she paused. Her neck joint extended upward and her head spun slowly all the way around. Belle was so absorbed in her work that she didn't notice Melody's movements until she tried to hand the android another dust filled bubble.

"What are you doing?" Belle asked.

"Silence," Melody said. Her eyes turned dark red. She was scanning the area.

Belle's heart skipped a beat. Melody rarely gave orders like that. She stood very still and tried to listen for what had alerted the android. She heard the turkens squawking as they shoved each other away from the feeding bowls. Outside, an alpaca shrieked. There was a shuffling sound just beyond the rear barn door, but that wasn't anything unusual. Then she heard it.

Something was whining outside the barn.

Belle froze. In the summer, she'd had an encounter with some fierce predators. They were huge and scary, with long, sharp teeth and glowing eyes. She'd thought of them as wolves. After that first encounter, she'd done some research about the animals' origins. A long time ago, humans had created hybrids — animals that were part dog and part wolf. They wanted pet dogs that could better survive on Mars. But some of the animals got loose, and their descendants had lived in the wild ever since. And like almost every other animal on Mars, these creatures grew enormous. That's why they looked more like wolves than dogs. They were terrifying when hungry or scared.

"Wolves?" Belle asked. She still thought of them that way.

Melody's red eyes turned yellow, which meant that she was still analyzing the sound. "Just one."

"I don't want it to kill any of the chicks."

The creature whined again. This time it sounded long and very sad. Curious about the animal and wanting to help if it was hurt, Belle moved to the back door.

"Wait!" Melody called.

Belle cracked open the door and peeked through the gap. There was a wolf, a wild dog, sitting out there. It was gray and scruffy, and one ear looked like it had been chewed up. Belle's heart jumped to her throat. Quickly, she considered how fast she could get to one of her hidden Petripuffs. If the dog showed its teeth, she'd freeze it and run back to the house.

Belle took a step back. The dog whined again. It was such a sad sound. She peeked at it again. The dog's tongue hung out of its mouth. It was panting heavily. She pushed the door open wider. When the dog saw her, it lowered its head. Then it lay down. It seemed that the dog wasn't here to attack Belle or her birds.

"I think it's thirsty," Belle said quietly and slowly, so she wouldn't scare it. "It doesn't look dangerous."

"Famous last words," Melody said.

"Get me some water, please. In a bowl or something."

"Why do you insist on taking such risky actions?" The android brought over a bowl filled with water.

Very carefully, Belle moved to the dog and set the bowl down an arm's length from its head. The dog moved closer and sniffed at the water. For several seconds, the only sound was that of the dog's tongue lapping up water. When the bowl was empty, it looked up at Belle and shook itself. Belle stepped back but was splattered anyway.

"Eew!" she laughed. "Dog drool!"

"You forget that this is a wild animal," Melody said, moving to stand between Belle and the dog.

Belle walked around her android. "It seems friendly. Look, it's wagging its tail."

"That alone is not a sign of tameness."

The dog took a step forward, lowering its head. Belle moved closer, holding her open hands out toward it. The dog sniffed her hands and then licked one palm. Belle giggled. She scratched the dog on its chin. It rubbed its face on her hand and then rolled over on its side.

"It is a male dog," Melody said.

"He's tame!" Belle rubbed his tummy. "I wonder who he belongs to?"

Melody's eyes went red again as she scanned the dog. "There are no implanted microchips or any other sign that he belongs to a person."

"Wait right here," Belle said to the dog. It stayed in position, as if it understood her.

Belle hurried into the barn and scooped up some mealworms. From her last encounter, she remembered that

the wild dogs liked to eat worms. They also liked turkens, but she wasn't going to sacrifice any of hers. Not this time.

Belle tried not to squirm as the dog chomped down hungrily on the worms. When he was done, she petted him again.

"Do you think we could keep him?" she asked.

"It is highly unlikely that your parents would approve," Melody said.

"I've always wanted a dog." Belle picked up a stick and threw it.

The dog jumped to its feet and ran to get it. He trotted back to her with the stick in his mouth. Belle threw it again and again, and each time the dog brought it back.

"His behavior indicates he must belong to someone," Melody said. "I shall search all media for requests to find a lost dog."

"Okay, but if no one claims him, I'm keeping him."

Belle threw the stick again.

"I hear something," Melody said.

The dog reached the place where the stick fell and stopped. It pricked up its ears.

"What is it?" Belle asked.

"A whistle, outside the range of human hearing," Melody replied. "There it is again."

The dog cocked its head to one side. He whined, looked back at Belle for a second, and then took off.

"Wait!" Belle ran after it.

"Belle!" Melody followed after Belle. "He is being called home. You cannot hear it, but I can."

Belle turned back to Melody. "We have to make sure he gets home safely. I want to know who owns him."

Belle took off after the dog. Melody rose into the air to follow her.

"This is not a wise decision," she said. "Your parents will be angry."

Belle pretended not to hear her android. She was determined to find out where this dog lived. She pushed her legs to go faster. In the distance, she caught sight of the dog's tail. He looked back at her and barked once, as if he was asking her to chase him.

So she did.

CHAPTER SEVEN

A MAJOR DISCOVERY

If it had been dark, Belle would've stopped the chase much sooner. But because the sun was shining, she didn't think twice about entering the forest across from their farmland. She followed the dog through the thick trees, hopping over bulging roots and skipping around wide ferns and prickly branches. Somewhere behind her she heard Melody hovering. That sound gave her the courage to keep going. Her android wouldn't let anything bad happen to her.

Emerging from the trees, Belle blinked in the bright sunlight. All she could see were more farms. She heard the dog panting and ran on. Melody followed, complaining occasionally. She caught a glimpse of the dog as he turned left and ran down a path by some tall hedges. She turned to follow. As she rounded the corner, the path seemed to go on forever. The dog had disappeared, leaving only a few tracks in the dusty ground. Alongside the path was a small stream. It seemed to emerge from nowhere, perhaps from underground.

"Belle, this is far enough," Melody said.

"I think he's almost home." Belle didn't take her eyes off the direction she thought the dog had taken.

She kept going, past several empty fields.

"You are the most stubborn human I have ever met," Melody said.

Belle stopped. She had completely lost sight of the dog. There weren't any tracks either. Her heart sank.

"I can't lose him now," she panted, her hands resting on her knees.

Melody made a creaking noise. She extended her head upward about two feet to scan the area. "I hear the whistle again. It is coming from the northeast, roughly two kilometers from here."

Belle looked up at her android. "I thought you wanted me to go home."

"Well, since we're here . . ." Melody said, throwing her hands up to imitate human behavior.

Belle held up her hand. "First, I need a drink." She bent down by the stream and cupped her hands.

"I don't think —" Melody began.

But Belle wasn't listening. She scooped a handful of water into her mouth, and then spat it back out.

"Yuck!" She spat several more times. "It's so salty!"

Melody walked over, opened one of her storage compartments, and offered Belle a bottle of water. "I believe your mother has mentioned before that the water on Mars is salty. It is why we have desalination plants in every town."

Belle gulped the fresh, clean water. "Thanks for waiting to remind me," she said sarcastically.

Someone in the distance shouted. Belle choked on her water. Melody put a finger to her mouth, which was a flat line that glowed red. She was in stealth mode.

"The barn ahead is registered as abandoned," she said in a low volume. "Yet, I detect many people present. And dogs."

Melody hovered ahead of Belle to see the open space beyond the edge of the hedgerow. Belle caught up to the android and peeked around her.

"What is it?" she asked.

"I recognize those vehicles from the raid on our farm," Melody responded.

"Raiders?" Belle whipped back behind the hedge. "Raiders are here? Have they seen us?"

"I do not believe so," Melody said. "But I believe the dog belongs to them."

Melody scanned the area, and then turned to face Belle. "We should leave immediately. I will contact the authorities to alert them of the raiders' location."

Belle nodded. She'd found the raiders' hideout. Her parents would be so pleased. She took a moment to catch her breath. But as she turned to follow Melody home, a warm, wet nose nudged her leg.

"Dog!" She gave the dog a hug as he licked her face. "I'm glad you've found your home, but your master is not a good person."

Someone whistled. Belle heard it this time. Then she heard the crunch of pebbles beneath boots. The footsteps were coming this way! Melody stepped in front of Belle to protect her. The dog licked Melody.

"Come on, boy!" a voice shouted.

The footsteps grew closer. Belle and Melody edged quietly away from the hedgerow. The dog followed them.

"Come here, you stupid dog!" The voice was gruff.

Belle froze. This was it. She'd be discovered by raiders. And who knew what they'd do to her? Her parents would be so mad.

Melody opened her side storage compartment and produced the livestock prod that she carried there. She held it ready.

The dog looked at Belle and cocked its head to the side. Then he turned and ran to his master. Belle let out the breath she was holding in.

"Come on now, boy. Let's go," Belle heard the voice say. Then she heard footsteps walking away.

"Wait a minute," Belle whispered, more to herself than to Melody. "The raiders have dogs. But Nabians don't keep pets. They consider them unsanitary."

Belle couldn't resist — she had to see for herself. She crept to the end of the hedgerow and peeked around the corner.

The raider walking next to the dog was human! Not Nabian, as everyone suspected.

Wait until her parents found out!

CHAPTER EIGHT
:GROUNDED:

Melody led the way home. By the time they arrived, it was evening. Before she even saw her farm, Belle heard her parents calling for her. They sounded frantic, as if they'd been calling for hours. Belle swallowed hard. She knew she was in big trouble.

But she was certain that once her parents learned that she'd discovered the raiders' hideout, they'd be so proud of her.

"Here I am!" She ran to her mom.

Yun and Zara hugged her and then started to yell at her.

"Do you know how dangerous it is out here?" Yun asked.

"How can you run off without telling us?" Zara said. The anger and fear were obvious in her voice.

"We found the barn door open and you were missing," Yun said.

"You gave us a terrible scare," Zara said.

"But you know I have Melody," Belle said. "Nothing will go wrong if she's with me."

Yun wiped his sweaty face. "I wish that were true."

Belle tried hard to calm her racing heart. "I have something important to tell you," she said.

Zara shook her head. "No more talk. You're grounded."

"That's right, young lady," Yun said. "You've given us enough worry for one day."

"But, I found it . . ." Belle began. Her mom raised her hand to stop Belle. Her dad turned away to lock up the barn.

"That's enough," Zara said. "Your dad and I are going to visit the Park family. They're really worried about the raids, so we're going to help them secure their water tanks."

Yun walked back and bent down to meet Belle's eyes. "You head straight to your room and don't come out until we get home. Do you understand me?"

"But —"

"No 'buts,'" Zara interrupted. Her parents wouldn't hear another word.

The words she needed to tell her parents were stuck in her throat. She wanted to explode with the news. But every time she tried, she was shut down. When they got back to the house she ran to her room and slammed her door shut. She heard her parents ordering Melody to keep an eye on Belle and to not let her out of her sight.

"We'll be back late," Zara said. "And we need to trust that Belle is in good hands."

Melody didn't reply. She had to obey. That's what androids did.

Sol 114/ Autumn, Mars Cycle 105

I am fuming mad! Mom and Dad wouldn't even let me talk!

They just can't believe a child would have the answers to their problems. Just because I'm 12. When will they start to take me seriously?

I can't believe they grounded me. Melody won't let me out of my room. She tried telling me bad jokes to cheer me up, but I didn't hear a word she said.

Sol 115/ Autumn, Mars Cycle 105

I'm still grounded. Mom and Dad won't even let me go above ground. And they won't let me tell them what I know. This is awful! At least the PF-51 arrived and I've finished making more puffs. But what good will they be if I can't get out?

Sol 116/Autumn, Mars Cycle 105

I'm so, so, so, bored! I've been stuck in the house for two whole days. I don't think I remember what sunlight looks like!

Melody said she reported the location of the raiders' hideout but nothing has been done so far. So that means they didn't believe her.

I have to get out of here and get proof. But how?

DING – DONG!

Belle looked up at the sound. Someone was ringing the doorbell. Finally! After two days of being grounded, she was desperate for a visitor. Her parents were acting so unreasonable. They refused to hear a word from her about her discovery. Every time she started to say something, they talked on and on about how dangerous Mars was.

"Melody, who is it?" Belle called from her bed. Her parents were out again. They were becoming the most popular parents in the area. Belle couldn't figure out why.

"It appears to be Lucas Walker," Melody said.

Belle jumped out of bed and ran to the front door.

"Mom said I can't go out, but she didn't say anything about others coming in," she said.

"Belle! Are you here?" a boy's voice called.

Belle unlocked the door. Ta'al stood there beside Lucas.

"Ta'al!" Belle was so happy to see them both.

"Our parents are all at the Parks' house again," Ta'al said. "Their farm was raided last night."

Belle's jaw dropped. Her parents hadn't said a word about that. Why were they keeping secrets from her?

"We got bored at their meeting," Lucas said.

"It's not the same without you there," Ta'al said.

Belle told them about being grounded. "But you have to hear what I found out!"

Lucas and Ta'al were captivated as Belle told them about her adventure chasing the dog. Then she surprised them with the information about the raiders' hideout.

"No way!" Lucas said.

"But if Melody told the Protectors, why haven't they done anything?" Ta'al said.

Melody brought them a tray full of snacks. "According to the authorities' site, they investigate tips from the public in the order they are received," she said. "Apparently, there have been a lot of recent raider attacks."

The three friends munched on their snacks in silence, each in deep thought.

"By the time the Protector gets to the raiders' hideout, they could be long gone," Lucas said. "They might already be gone. It's been two days."

"But it's in the hands of the authorities now," Ta'al said. "There's nothing we can do."

Belle looked at her two friends. "Nothing? Are you sure?" An idea was growing in her head.

Belle stood up quickly and grabbed her bag hanging on the wall. Then she went to her closet and began stuffing the bag with Petripuffs. "Do you have any of your gel pellets here?" she asked Lucas.

"Yeah, some," he replied, pulling some pellets from his pocket. "I usually carry some with me, just in case."

"Ta'al, do you have your sonic disrupter with you?" Belle asked her friend.

"Yes, it's in my bag, along with some spare hearing protection," Ta'al said. "With all of the raider activity, I thought it best to bring it along on our way here."

"Good," Belle said. "Because we're going to get some proof to show where the raiders are hiding. Then our parents will have to listen to us."

"I cannot allow that," Melody said. "Your parents gave strict orders that you are to stay here."

"But that was days ago Melody," Belle argued. "I've been stuck in this room for two days already. Mom and Dad didn't say how long I should be grounded. I think I've served my sentence."

"You make a logical argument," Melody said. "But I do not think you should leave the house without any adult supervision."

"That's why you should come with us. Besides, we need you to come along and record what we see as proof," Belle argued. "Our parents might not listen to us. But they'll believe you, especially when you show them a recording of the raiders' hideout."

"I see that no matter what I say, you will do exactly as you please," Melody said. She proceeded to load up her central storage compartment with water bottles and a first aid kit.

Belle hugged her android. "As long as you're with us, I know we'll be safe."

CHAPTER NINE
:A DANGEROUS:
PLAN

Trudging through the forest in the evening was scarier than it was a few mornings ago. The trees felt much closer together, and the air was damp. Belle's feet kept sinking into the forest floor, coating her shoes with ice-cold mud. Even Ta'al, who was usually so graceful, stumbled a couple of times. Lucas, however, was too excited about their mission. He ran through the forest faster than all of them.

"Be careful not to drop any puffs!" Belle warned him.

By the time they emerged from the forest, the sky was dark. The moon Phobos only provided a dim glow. It was barely enough to light their way through the paths. Melody was careful to keep her eye lamps dim, just in case there were raiders around.

Just past the salty stream, Belle crouched down and signaled for the others to do the same. Melody dimmed her light beams even lower, and they leaned against the hedges, listening for the raiders' voices.

At first, everything was silent.

"Maybe they've moved on," Ta'al whispered.

"I knew it. We're too late!" Lucas said.

They stood up to stretch their cramped legs. But then the sudden boom of a loud engine made them jump. It was followed by whoops and laughter. Something began to rumble, sounding like a giant with a bellyache.

"That's a pump," Lucas said. "They must be filling a water tank."

"Do you think it's the Parks' water?" Belle asked.

"We should contact the authorities," Ta'al said. "I don't think we can handle this ourselves."

Melody's large eyes turned a light blue color. She was sending a communication to the Protector. "It is done," she said. "Now we should head home."

"Wait," Belle said. "There's something you two need to see first."

Belle stepped to the end of the hedgerow and poked her head around. She waved for her friends to do the same.

In front of the abandoned barn stood at least a dozen raiders. They stood in a semi-circle, cheering as their truck unloaded a tankful of water into the ground. The raiders were draped in layers of coats and cloaks. Every part of their bodies was covered.

Drats! Belle needed them to remove their headpieces to prove to Lucas that the Nabians weren't the enemy.

"Okay, we saw them," Lucas said. "Now let's go."

"Oh!" Ta'al suddenly gasped.

Belle whipped around to see her friend standing with her hand over her mouth. Ta'al's eyes were wide and almost completely black.

"Look over in the corner, there," Ta'al said, pointing to a small group of people on the far end of the pump.

Belle and Lucas squinted. Nabians! Four of them, standing and watching. Belle's heart dropped to her feet. Had Lucas been right all along?

As the water continued to be pumped, it seemed as if the raiders became bored. The group began to break up, and one raider unwound the scarves around his head.

He was human. He walked over to a pile of sticks and got a fire going. Others were attracted to the fire's warmth and gathered around it. They too removed their scarves. More humans. The only ones who didn't move to the fire were the Nabians.

Maybe they weren't cold? Then Belle looked at Ta'al. She had her arms wrapped around herself. Ta'al looked cold. So why did it seem that the others weren't interested in the warm fire?

"*Hantu* — wait!" Ta'al said. "Those Nabians are not a part of the raiders."

Belle stretched over Lucas to get a better look. Ta'al was right. The reason the Nabians hadn't moved was right behind them. Two large raiders, still wrapped in cloaks and scarves, were holding blasters pointed at the Nabians.

"They're prisoners!" Belle said in a hoarse whisper.

"I know them," Ta'al said. "They're the ones who've been missing." She hadn't taken her eyes off the Nabians. "We have to save them."

"We can't do anything," Lucas said. "Those guards have blasters."

"They're moving," Belle said.

The raiders with the blasters prodded the Nabians in the back. The prisoners shuffled ahead, slowly and clumsily.

"Their feet are chained," Ta'al said. Her voice rose with each word. Belle put a finger to her lips to remind her friend to stay quiet.

The prisoners were herded toward a tent to the far left of the tanker truck. The raider guards checked the restraints on the Nabians before shoving them into the tent. They secured the entrance, then walked over to the fire.

Belle shivered. She wasn't sure if it was because of the cold or what she'd just seen. She'd proven her point. Perhaps it was now time to let the adults take over. She moved away from the hedge and gestured for her friends to follow. They'd only taken a few steps when they heard someone wail.

The cry echoed through the chilly night air. Belle felt like it stabbed her right in her chest.

"What was that?" she said.

They all froze in place.

"From the sounds I am hearing," Melody said, turning to scan the scene beyond the hedges, "there are dogs in the tent with the prisoners."

"No!" Ta'al said. She had her hands over her ears and was shivering. Was it fear or anger, or both?

Standing in the cold and listening to the wailing of the prisoners, Belle knew they had to do something. They couldn't wait for the Protector.

"We'll sneak around the camp, behind the tent," Belle said. "Melody can cut an opening in the material. Right?" She looked at her android.

"I can use my laser to burn a hole in it," Melody said.

Belle nodded. "We can save the prisoners, at least."

Ta'al nodded so hard it looked like her head might fall off.

"No, we should wait," Lucas said. "We could make things worse."

"I agree with Lucas," Melody said. "I am not prepared to sacrifice your safety, Belle."

Belle wasn't listening to either of them. She shoved plugs into her ears, and then pulled out two Petripuffs. Ta'al held her disruptor at the ready.

"Lucas, you stay here and be our lookout," Belle said. "If the raiders decide to head our way, try to distract them. Make some noise, and then get out of here. We'll meet at the entrance to the forest."

She turned to Melody. "You'll come with us, okay?"

Melody's eyes and mouth went red. Belle smiled. Her android was in stealth mode.

CHAPTER TEN
A DARING RESCUE

Belle and Ta'al waited for Melody to signal that all of
the raiders were looking away from the hedges. Crouching
low, the girls dashed across the path to the hedgerow on the
other side. They ran to the end of that path and stopped to
listen. They were closer to the captives' tent now — so close
they could hear dogs snarling and more wailing.

Belle didn't want to think about what was going on inside. She just knew that they had to do whatever they could to help the prisoners. She didn't want to think about the danger or how angry her parents would be if they knew what she was doing. Or worse, how awful it would be to get caught by the raiders. But she pressed on in spite of her fears.

The last dash to the tent was going to be out in the open. They had to stay low and run one at a time. Melody went first. Hovering with all her lights turned off, she was almost invisible in the dark. Belle wished she had that power. She was glad that she was at least wearing dark colors. Ta'al, though, was wearing a lot of bright yellow and pink clothing.

"You go next," Belle said to her friend. "When Melody signals, run fast."

Ta'al tucked in all the loose fabric around her middle. Then she began rubbing the outer layer of clothing with both hands. As she did, the fabric changed color. Within seconds, she was cloaked in darkness.

"Clever," Belle said. Ta'al grinned. Nabian technology was incredible.

Ta'al dashed over to Melody like a ghost. Belle could barely see her. Then it was her turn. She took a deep breath and swallowed her fear. With her eyes fixed on the one tiny red light on Melody's head, she ran.

Belle took several large leaps. But because of Mars' lower gravity, her legs sent her flying higher than the corral posts. In the distance, someone shouted. She couldn't hear the exact words. Then more people were shouting. She hit the ground and crouched down behind a post that was too narrow to hide her. Her heart pounded so hard in her chest that she couldn't hear anything else. She pulled out an earplug and opened her eyes.

The raiders had abandoned their fire and were running. Belle stretched up a little to get a better look. *Were they coming for her?*

"Belle! Run to me!" She heard Melody call.

It took all her strength to force her legs to keep moving. But she did until she collapsed into Melody's hard arms.

"Should we run?" she said, in half breaths.

"Lucas must have made a distraction, like you asked," Ta'al said.

"They are headed the other way," Melody confirmed.

Belle let out her breath. Lucas was doing a great job. She leaned up against the side of the tent to catch her breath. Meanwhile, Ta'al had her ear up against the tent wall. She waved Belle and Melody over to her side.

"This might be a safe place to cut through the fabric," Ta'al whispered. "I don't hear anything on the other side."

Melody agreed and pulled out a small laser. Belle held on to her Petripuffs, ready to throw them at the dogs inside the tent.

"There's one guard left on the other side," Ta'al said. "Give me some of your puffs. As soon as you're through, I'll paralyze him." Ta'al moved around the side of the tent and took a stance, ready to take action.

Melody's laser burned through the fabric, scorching it like fire. Immediately they heard sniffing sounds and low snarling. Belle heard Ta'al huff as she hurled a Petripuff at the guard. He cried out briefly, and then there was silence.

As soon as a flap was cut through the tent wall, Belle caught a peek inside. Two angry wolf-dogs stood ready to attack them. Belle lobbed a puff at each dog. The first dog fell immediately, yelping pitifully. But the other puff missed its mark. The second dog jumped through the hole. Baring its teeth, it pounced at Belle.

Belle crouched on the ground and covered her head with her arms. She squeezed her eyes shut and braced herself for the pain. Why had she chosen to do such a stupid thing? How would this night end?

Nothing happened. She waited a few seconds, in case she'd misjudged the dog's attack.

She opened her eyes to see the dog lying on the ground, just inches from where she crouched. Ta'al stood on the other side of the dog, looking terrified. In one hand, she held her disruptor. She held her other hand in front of her, frozen in position after throwing a puff at the attacking dog.

Belle stood up with wobbly legs. She gave her friend a thumbs-up. Ta'al didn't respond. She kept staring at the dog.

"I've never harmed a living thing in my life," Ta'al said shakily. "And already tonight, I've hurt two."

"Don't worry. They'll be fine in a few minutes," Belle said, trying to sound confident, and failing. "I designed the puffs so they wouldn't do any permanent damage to anyone."

Melody had already stepped inside the tent. She was using her laser to cut the shackles off the prisoners. They were speechless at what was happening.

Belle began helping the Nabians out of the tent, one by one. As the first one emerged, Ta'al spoke to them in their language.

"This was too dangerous for you," one of the Nabians said in the common language, so that Belle understood too.

"You should have just told the authorities," another said.

"We couldn't let you suffer while we waited," Belle said. "We don't know how long it would have taken the Protector to arrive."

"*Sia-mi* — thank you." The Nabians patted Belle on the back. She could see the cuts and scrapes on their skin, even in the darkness.

"We should move," Melody reminded them all.

"We'll head this way," the first Nabian said, pointing away from where Lucas was waiting for them. "Our homes are in this direction."

"All right," Belle said. "But please tell the authorities what happened as soon as you can."

The Nabians nodded, giving Belle and then Ta'al an odd look. Ta'al nodded back with an expression that said she understood their meaning. Belle was confused. But there wasn't time to ask questions. They had to get back and meet up with Lucas.

They ran back the way they'd come. The raiders were nowhere to be seen. Where did they all go? Had they simply run off at Lucas' distraction?

The pump engine was still humming when they reached the place where they'd left Lucas. He wasn't there. He must have moved on to the forest.

But when they reached the forest meeting point, Lucas wasn't there either. They called out cautiously, but there was no reply.

"We lost his tracks a while back," Melody said. "Perhaps he took a different way into the forest."

"Or maybe he went to your house?" Ta'al said.

Belle didn't like this one bit. Something wasn't right. Lucas wouldn't change the plan like that, would he? But Ta'al had a point. They hadn't planned for this possibility. Surely Lucas would head to her house.

They ran on as fast as they could. As they crossed through Belle's farm gate, she fully expected to see a smiling Lucas sitting on her porch step, wondering what had taken them so long.

But the porch was empty.

Belle's stomach twisted. *What if something had happened to Lucas?*

"Melody, call Lucas' home," she said. "See if he's there."

"No one is answering," Melody said. "They're all at the Parks' house tonight."

Belle took off in the direction of the Parks' farm. It was on her way to school, and she knew all the short cuts.

They ran through the backfields and around the small barn where their horsel, Loki, slept.

When they reached the Parks' house, the meeting had finished and all the parents were on their way out.

"What are you doing here, Belle?" Yun said, startled.

It took Belle a full minute to catch her breath. She was almost in a full panic. Most of her words were garbled. Once again, it was Ta'al's calmness that saved the moment.

Ta'al explained what they'd done. With each sentence, more neighbors gathered. Gasps of horror filled the air around them.

"And now we can't find Lucas," Ta'al ended. "We need your help."

Myra broke down crying and fell into Paddy's arms. He looked pale.

"The raiders have our son!" he said. "Show us the hideout. We have to get him back."

Every neighbor stood ready to help. There was a lot of shouting and cursing.

"Wait!" Yun said, waving his arms. "We need to calm down and think for a moment."

People quieted, but Myra was weeping loudly. Zara went to her side.

"The Protector left our meeting in a hurry, didn't he?" Yun said. "Perhaps that's when he received Melody's call. So that's good news. The authorities are on their way."

"Yes, but those raiders would've been alerted when they found our boy," Paddy said, getting redder in the face with every word. "We have to go now!"

Yun nodded. "I agree, but let's be smart about this."

"We'll need a wagon," Zara said. "It'll be faster."

Mr. Park hitched his wagon to two giant horsels and everyone piled in. Yun and Zara insisted that Ta'al and Belle sit inside the wagon while Melody directed Mr. Park to the raiders' hideout.

The ride was bumpy as the horsels ran as fast as they could. The wagon was packed with neighbors. They all looked at Ta'al and Belle as if they were the naughtiest girls on the planet.

Belle felt like she could cry at any moment. But she was determined not to show any tears in front of the others. This had been her mistake. She had been so stupid to think that she could solve the raider problem herself. What did she think would happen? That she and her friends would catch the raiders, free the Nabians, and be hailed as heroes?

However this night turned out, she was sure the adults would always see her as a foolish, disobedient child.

CHAPTER ELEVEN

:SAVING A FRIEND:

The wagon stopped just outside the abandoned farm that served as the raiders' hideout. Quietly, everyone stepped out and formed into groups of three or four. Some of the farmers were armed with blasters. Others just held sticks and shovels.

"You two stay inside the wagon," Yun warned Belle. "And I mean it."

Belle couldn't look her dad in the eye. She blamed herself for this mess. Ta'al was silent. Her parents were among the neighbors getting ready to save Lucas too. They hadn't said a word to her this whole time. Belle wondered if that was worse than being scolded.

"Do you understand me, Belle?" her dad asked.

Belle nodded, looking at her feet. She hated the idea of not being able to do something — anything — to fix her mistake and save her friend.

She and Ta'al stood through the small window at the raiders' barn. Everything was silent now, eerie under the cloak of night. Even the sound of the water pump was gone. Had the raiders moved on so quickly?

"There!" Belle heard someone say. Her gaze turned to where everyone else was looking.

The Protector, with its bright-red scanning eye emerged from the barn ahead. Belle was surprised at how quietly the large android moved. She and Ta'al pressed their ears against the window so they could hear the conversation with the big android.

"There is no one in the area," the Protector said. "But there is evidence of recent human activity here."

Several murmurs of "Human?" arose from the crowd.

"Where can they have gone?" Paddy shouted at the Protector. "They have our son!"

The Protector pointed to the sky. "The drones are scanning the area. We should have results soon."

"That's not good enough," Paddy said, looking around at the others. "I'm forming a search party. Who's with me?"

Everyone voiced their support. Paddy proceeded to organize people into groups. Each group moved off in a different direction. Melody was instructed to stay, with strict orders not to let Belle or Ta'al leave the wagon.

Belle collapsed into a seat. She dropped her head into her hands. Ta'al sat next to her and stroked her back soothingly.

"He'll be fine," Ta'al said. "They can't have gone far." Belle could hear the uncertainty in her friend's voice. But she appreciated her for trying to help.

The horsels whinnied. Belle looked up. The big creatures stomped their hooves. Then something yelped. Belle jumped up and stuck her head out the front of the wagon. There, next to the horsels stood a dog with one chewed up ear — her dog! The one she'd found and followed. She'd know him anywhere.

"Melody, look!"

Melody was already coming around the wagon. The dog trotted up to her and gave her a lick.

"You are right," she said. "It is our friend, the dog."

The dog turned its head and whined. Belle knew what that meant.

"Do you hear the whistle?" she asked Melody.

"I do," she said. "It is coming from the south."

"Melody, you know what this means, don't you?" Belle said. "We have to follow the dog. It can lead us to Lucas!"

Belle climbed down from the wagon, followed by Ta'al. Belle stroked the dog's head, then held on to the thick fur around his neck. He whined again. His owner was calling him.

The dog struggled against Belle's grip. Not wanting to hurt him, she let go. He took off.

"You stay here, while I follow him," Melody said. "I will inform your father."

Belle watched as Melody and the dog faded into the darkness. She wasn't sure what to do. She didn't want to disobey her parents again. After all, her impulsive actions had gotten Lucas into trouble in the first place.

Belle turned to Ta'al. She didn't have to say anything. The determined expression on Ta'al's face told her what she needed to do.

"I still have my disruptor and one puff," Ta'al said, patting her pocket.

Belle nodded and set her jaw. She'd gotten Lucas into this, and she was going to get him out. "Right. Let's go."

At first, the girls followed the sound of Melody's mechanical feet trudging over the rough ground. Then they heard the approaching footsteps of a search party. Everyone had received Melody's message and were gathering for a showdown with the raiders. Belle and Ta'al hid as well as they could, staying far enough behind not to be seen.

They climbed a nearby tree and lay still to watch. In the distance was a circle of vehicles and several shadowy figures. Dogs barked and howled as raiders spoke in harsh tones. They didn't see the farmers circling around them. The Protector was nowhere to be seen.

Suddenly the farmers let out a loud cry and charged. The raiders were stunned, but only for a moment. A blaster went off. Belle cringed.

"We have to help," she said.

Ta'al was already climbing down. They hit the ground and ran into the fray. The scene was chaotic, with raiders and farmers tangled in a messy fight. Dogs growled and barked, but most of them ran away as soon as blaster fire was heard.

Belle signaled to Ta'al to circle around the chaos and head for a small nearby barn. Light poured through the bottom of the door.

"I bet Lucas is being held in there," Belle said.

They were almost there when a large raider stepped in front of them.

"Where do you think you're going?" he roared.

Belle and Ta'al froze. The raider was a mountain of a man, with dark curly hair that stuck out everywhere. He reached out his hand and grabbed Ta'al by the cuff of her cloak. He wore gloves with the fingers cut out and he smelled like old fuel. With his other hand, he pulled Belle off the ground by her jacket. She kicked him with all her might but he just laughed. Both girls screamed.

Belle's arms flailed helplessly until one hand smacked against her pocket. Inside was her last Petripuff!

"Hold your breath!" she shouted to Ta'al as she lobbed the puff at the man's chest.

The puff hit its mark, releasing its white powder into the big raider's face. He let go of Ta'al and dropped Belle, who fell to the ground on her knees. Although her skin burned, she dared not take a breath. Belle crawled as far away from the man as she could. He choked and gagged, then fell to his knees. He collapsed onto his side, eyes wide open in disbelief. He couldn't move a muscle.

Belle scrambled to her feet and ran for the barn door before she dared to breathe again. She pried open the door.

"I have one more puff," Ta'al whispered. "But I also have my disruptor."

The girls shoved the earplugs into their ears, and then Belle swung the barn door open.

Lucas sat crouched on the floor of the old barn. His hands and feet were bound with rope. But he was alone. The raiders were all outside fighting the farmers.

"I'm so sorry," Belle said as she looked for something to cut the ropes. She found a rusty old saw blade and began cutting him loose. "Are you all right? Did they hurt you?"

Lucas shook his head. His face was streaked with dried tears and dirt. He looked too frightened to even speak. Ta'al helped lift him to his feet as soon as he was free. Together, the three ran back to the barn door.

But suddenly the same mountainous raider appeared at the door in front of them. He'd recovered from the Petripuff and looked furious.

"Nice try, little ones," he growled. "But it takes more than some kiddie powder to stop me."

He lunged at them, hands stretched out, trying to grab anyone within his reach. Belle jumped out of his way, as did Ta'al. But Lucas was too slow. The man grabbed him and yanked him off the floor so his feet were dangling.

"Please put me down!" Lucas cried.

Belle looked at Ta'al. Her friend looked back and nodded. The girls instinctively knew what to do. Belle stepped up to the man.

"Don't you hurt him!" she screamed.

She looked right at Lucas. She placed her hands over her ears. Lucas seemed to understand. He imitated her. Then Ta'al pointed her sonic disruptor at the man and pushed the button. Belle only heard a shrill tone, thanks to her ear protection. Lucas squirmed, but the effect on the raider was worse. He yelped and dropped Lucas. He slapped his hands over his ears. And at that moment, Ta'al lobbed her last puff at him. The huge man didn't see the puff in time. It burst in his face, and he once again dropped to the ground — paralyzed.

Belle ran out of the barn with Lucas and Ta'al. Her heart was pounding. They were out of ammunition, and there were many more raiders to deal with. What would they do now?

They were greeted by bright lights shining from the sky above. Floodlights — and the sound of drones.

The Protector stood in the center of the floodlights. Every opening in its armor held some kind of weapon. The weapons all pointed at the raiders kneeling on the ground with their hands behind their heads. Farmers stood behind each one, pointing whatever weapons they had at the raiders.

"Lucas!" Myra cried as she came running. She hugged Lucas so hard, he started to laugh and cry at the same time.

Paddy soon joined his family in a group hug. Meanwhile, the drones dropped nets over each of the raiders. The drones lifted them into the air and carried them away.

After the drones left and the whole place fell into silence and darkness, Yun and Zara walked up to Belle. She expected to be yelled at by her parents for disobeying them again. But they too huddled into a group hug, and no one said a word.

"We're all safe," Yun finally said, as if he knew what Belle was thinking. "That's all that matters now."

Sol 117/Autumn, Mars Cycle 105, night

What a night! I'm still shaking from all that's happened. I just thank the universe that Lucas is safe. I feel so bad — this was all my fault. But no one has said anything to me about it. Right now, all the parents are just happy that we're safe and the raiders have been arrested. I want to go to sleep. I'm so tired. But my brain is racing. I keep replaying everything that's happened in my head. It's over. I just need to let that sink in.

Sol 118/Autumn, Mars Cycle 105, morning

I haven't slept this much in ages. When I woke up, it was almost lunchtime!

Dad says that now the raiders have been dealt with, we have to focus on fixing our tank and restocking it with new water. Ta'al's parents have generously offered to share their security technology with us, as well as any neighbor who wants it. They really are the nicest people. I feel so awful that I put Ta'al in danger too.

One good thing has happened though. I think Lucas may actually think of Ta'al as a friend now.

CHAPTER TWELVE
:RAIDER:
COMES HOME

"The raiders who were arrested will stand trial in Tharsis City," the Protector said. The huge android was meeting with the Songs, the Walkers, and Ta'al's family, who were gathered in Belle's house. "You may be asked to give testimony through holo-vid. But they will not bother you anymore."

"Thanks to our kids for discovering their hideout," Paddy said. His arm had been around Lucas the whole evening. Even though a week had passed, Paddy and Myra still hovered over Lucas like he might disappear any moment.

"But I hope you've learned your lesson," Yun added, turning to Belle. "Some adventures aren't safe for children."

"I'm not a child," Belle said. "I'm almost thirteen."

"Maybe so, but some adventures aren't safe for teens, either," Zara said.

Belle smiled at Ta'al and Lucas. They made a good team.

"I'm just grateful that no one was hurt," So'ark said. Ta'al's other parents nodded vigorously in agreement. "But I do admire your resourcefulness. We would be interested to study your Petripuffs. Perhaps we can make some improvements on the technology."

Belle beamed with pride.

"Maybe we can do that for our science fair project," Ta'al said. "Your puffs with some Nabian improvements."

"That's a great idea," Belle said. "It would be amazing if the Petripuffs won on Mars, like they did back on Earth."

She looked over at Lucas, who was watching them.

"Maybe both our projects could win," Belle said quickly. She didn't want to offend Lucas.

"You never know," he said with a laugh. "Ever since you showed up, so many things have changed."

"In a good way, I hope," she said.

He shrugged. "More like scary and exciting. You need me and Ta'al to keep you out of trouble."

"Wonderful," Melody said. "More mischief to contain."

Everyone laughed. Belle liked the sound of that. Lucas had begun to treat Ta'al as if they were all one group of close friends. Things were changing — for the better.

All three families walked outside with the Protector as he took his leave. After the big android was gone, Zara invited everyone back into the house for a light lunch. As they turned to head inside, Belle heard a whine.

There by the fence was her friend with the chewed-up ear. She ran toward him.

"Wait, Belle!" she heard her dad say. "It's a wild animal!"

"It's my dog!" Belle bent down and rubbed her face in its soft fur. The dog licked her face. "He must be missing his owner, now that he's in jail."

Belle led the dog to her family. He sat very still, panting, while everyone stared at him.

"He's friendly," Belle said. "Pet him and see."

One by one everyone petted the dog. Ta'al did too, but her parents just stood back and watched.

"He seems friendly enough," Yun said.

"Can we keep him?" Belle looked at her parents. "Please?"

Zara shook her head. "We don't have room in our home."

"What if we kept him in the above-ground front porch area?" Belle asked. "He could be a guard dog for us."

Zara and Yun looked at each other. The other parents were already smiling. They knew what the answer would be.

Belle squealed with delight when her parents agreed.

"What will you call him?" Lucas asked.

Belle thought for a while. She looked at the dog, who panted eagerly at his new owner. Then a huge smile spread across her face.

"I know exactly what his name is," she said. Her friends waited, excited to hear. Even the parents stopped chatting.

"His name is Raider."

Sol 125/Autumn, Mars Cycle 105

I have the pet I've always wanted. And all my friends and family are safe. Still, when I think of what we did, I shiver. Things could've gone so wrong. I think Mom and Dad know how bad I feel though. Thankfully, they've chosen not to punish me.

Tonight, Raider is sleeping above ground. He seemed happy when I left him with a large blanket, along with some food and water. I think over time, Mom and Dad will get used to him. Hopefully, he'll be sleeping in my room very soon.

ABOUT THE AUTHOR

A.L. Collins learned a lot about writing from her teachers at Hamline University in St. Paul, MN. She has always loved reading science fiction stories about other worlds and strange aliens. She enjoys creating and writing about new worlds, as well as envisioning what the future might look like. Since writing the Redworld series, she has collected a map of Mars that hangs in her living room and a rotating model of the red planet, which sits on her desk. When not writing, Collins enjoys spending her spare time reading and playing board games with her family. She lives near Seattle, Washington with her husband and five dogs.

• • • ● ● ● •

ABOUT THE ILLUSTRATOR

Tomislav Tikulin was born in Zagreb, Croatia. Tikulin has extensive experience creating digital artwork for book covers, posters, DVD jackets, and production illustrations. Tomislav especially enjoys illustrating tales of science fiction, fantasy, and scary stories. His work has also appeared in magazines such as *Fantasy & Science Fiction, Asimov's Science Fiction, Orson Scott Card's Intergalactic Medicine Show*, and *Analog Science Fiction & Fact*. Tomislav is also proud to say that his artwork has graced the covers of many books including Larry Niven's *The Ringworld Engineers*, Arthur C. Clarke's *Rendezvous With Rama*, and Ray Bradbury's *Dandelion Wine* (50th anniversary edition).

:WHAT DO YOU THINK?:

1. Lucas didn't like Ta'al at first because of the rumors he'd heard about the Nabian people. Why do you think Lucas believed the rumors? What could he have done differently to learn the truth about the Nabians?

2. The Songs and their neighbors joined together to help defeat the Water Raiders. Describe a time when you worked with your friends to accomplish something that helped everyone.

3. Belle disobeyed her parents several times in this story. Discuss three ways the events of the story would change if she had done what they said.

4. Belle has a great imagination, which helped her invent her Petripuffs. Do you have any ideas for cool new inventions? Write down your ideas and describe what each invention can do.

5. If you could have any animal as a pet, what would it be? Write about how you would take care of that pet and what life would be like with it in your home.

:GLOSSARY:

abandon (uh-BAN-duhn)—to leave and never return

auditory (AH-dih-toh-ree)—having to do with hearing or the ears

binary (BYE-nair-ee)—something made of or having two parts

classified (KLASS-uh-fide)—declared secret

condone (kuhn-DOHN)—to regard or treat something as acceptable, forgivable, or harmless

desalination (dee-sah-luh-NAY-shuhn)—the process of removing salt from ocean water

hybrid (HYE-brid)—a plant or animal that has been bred from two different species

ignorant (IG-nohr-uhnt)—lacking in knowledge or information

illogical (i-LOJ-uh-kuhl)—when something does not make sense

morale (moh-RAL)—the feelings or state of mind of a person or group of people

prejudice (PREJ-uh-diss)—an opinion about others that is unfair or not based on facts

unsanitary (uhn-SAN-i-ter-ee)—not clean or healthy

torso (TOR-soh)—the part of the body between the neck and waist, not including the arms

:MARS TERMS:

elixian (ee-LICKS-ee-uhn)—Nabian word meaning "equal partner"

gyrvel (guhr-VEL)—Nabian word meaning "welcome"

holo-vid (HOHL-uh-vid)—a holographic projection that shows videos for information or entertainment

horsel (HOHRSS-el)—a hybrid animal that is part horse and part camel, used as a work animal on Mars

matekap (MAH-teh-kap)—Nabian word meaning "sleepover"

Mars Cycle (MARS SY-kuhl)—the Martian year, equal to 687 Earth days, or 1.9 Earth years

Nabian (NAY-bee-uhn)—an advanced alien race with nose ridges and plastic-like hair; their eye color reflects their surroundings

shoat (SHOHT)—a hybrid animal that is part sheep and part goat; farmers on Mars raise them for their milk and wool

sia-mi (SEE-ah-MEE)—Nabian word meaning "thank you"

Sol (SOHL)—the name for the Martian day

Sulux (SUH-lux)—an alien race with purple skin and arm and neck ridges

Terran (TAIR-uhn)—a person or thing that is originally from Earth

turken (TUR-ken)—a hybrid bird that is part turkey and part chicken; farmers on Mars raise them for their eggs and meat

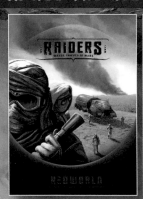